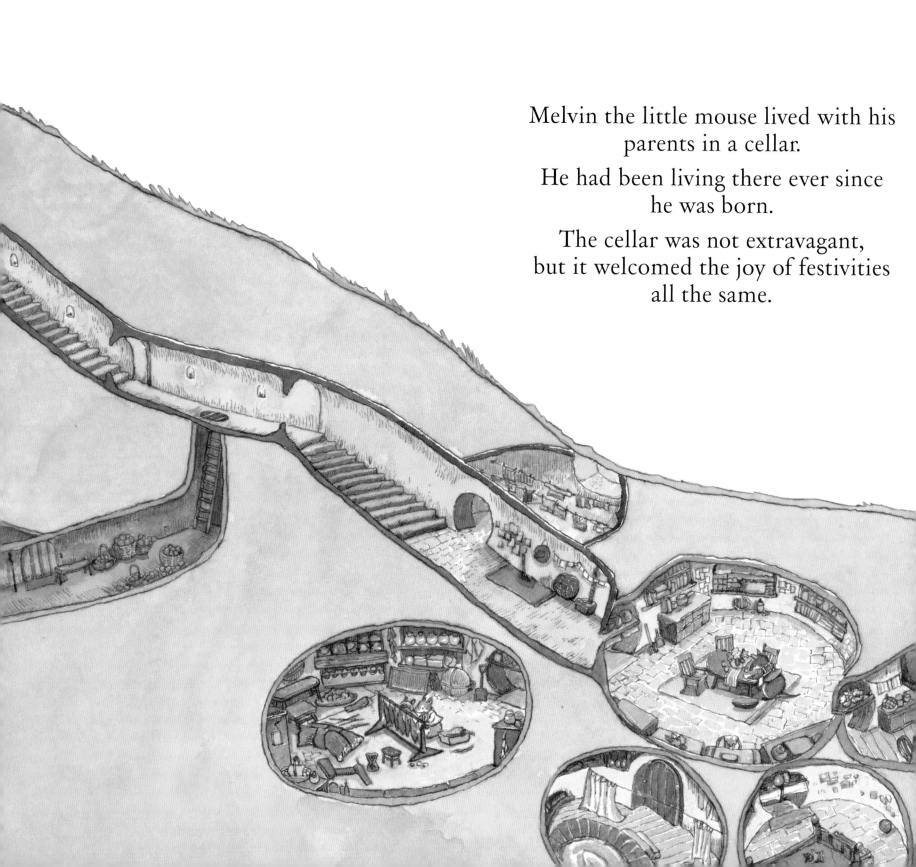

Melvin the little mouse lived with his
parents in a cellar.

He had been living there ever since
he was born.

The cellar was not extravagant,
but it welcomed the joy of festivities
all the same.

# When the Mice Family Comes to Visit

Written by Wenjun QIN
Illustrated by Xiaoxuan XU

As the annual Mice Festival drew near, the cellar was full of
excitement and joy.

Melvin's dad was busy writing invitations to their relatives. They
were hosting the family this year!

Melvin was tasked with adding drawings to the letters, and Mom
placed floral stamps on the envelopes.

"How wonderful it is to celebrate the festival with my beloved
relatives!" Melvin thought.

Dad went up the hill to pick wild fruit and flowers.
Mom hung strings of lanterns around the rooms.
Melvin took out his precious chocolate and quietly placed it around the living room.
The sweet scent of chocolate soon wafted through the air.

On the eve of the festival, Melvin and his parents were still busy preparing.
There were fragrant flowers and colorful candies everywhere, but most of all,
the cellar was filled with joy.

Dad said, "Buddy, let's have a sweet flower bath to get you ready."
Melvin squealed in excitement, "Oh, yes please!"

After his bath, Melvin plopped onto his bed. He imagined how lively the cellar would be tomorrow, and he became so excited that he tossed and turned.

But suddenly, he grew worried.

"What if there's a storm tomorrow?
What if our relatives decide not to come?" he murmured.

 "Honey, there's no need to worry," Mom reassured him. "Tomorrow will be a
joyous festival."
With his mom's comforting words, Melvin fell asleep and dreamed a sweet dream.

At dawn, everything was fine as Mom had promised. White clouds floated in the blue sky, and the sun was smiling sweetly.

Uncle John's big family showed up first.

Uncle John took Auntie Jenny's arm in his and led his sons along the road. There were a dozen boys.

Auntie Jenny presented her thoughtful gifts to Mom.

"These are just what we need!" Mom said gratefully. "An acorn cup to store rice, and a pottery cup to collect sweet spring raindrops. Thank you so much, dear!"

Then a fabulous pumpkin car thundered down the road. In it were Auntie Lily and Uncle Lane's big family. Their daughters wore sweet flowers in their hair and butterfly knots on their tails. The girls looked so pretty in their festival outfits.

Uncle Lane brought with him many bags with gifts. There were cakes, blueberries, sweet pine nut fudge, and all kinds of toys.

The little mice exchanged gifts. Melvin received a handkerchief and a small bottle of sesame oil from the girls and a piece of wild fruit and vegetables from the boys.

Melvin had prepared pencils, paintings, building blocks, and smooth pebbles to give his cousins.

Everyone cherished the gifts dearly.

From the door came a thunderous laugh.

Dad had brought Grandpa and Grandma here!

Grandma kissed and hugged each one of her grandchildren.

"Oh, sweeties!" Grandma called affectionately.

With so many kisses and hugs, the cellar was full of love and excitement.

Long-bearded Grandpa sat in a rocking chair, equally excited to see his grandchildren.
"I want to look around," he said. "My dear kids, would you please take me?"

All the little mice rushed forward to hold up Grandpa's rocking chair.

"I am the world's proudest grandpa!" bragged Grandpa. "Run fast, run fast, let's explore the rooms!"

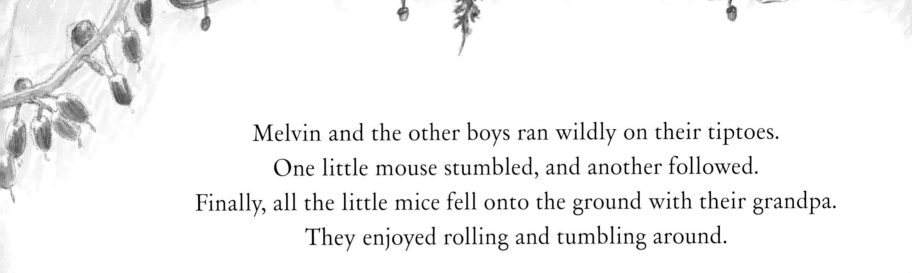

Melvin and the other boys ran wildly on their tiptoes.
One little mouse stumbled, and another followed.
Finally, all the little mice fell onto the ground with their grandpa.
They enjoyed rolling and tumbling around.

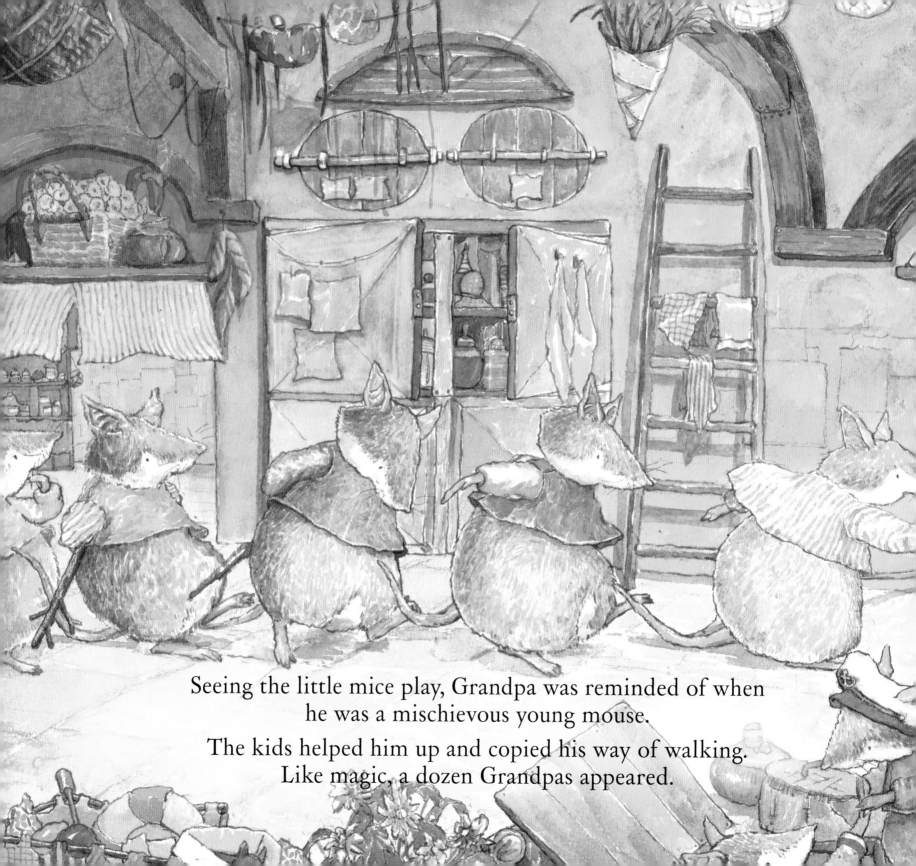

Seeing the little mice play, Grandpa was reminded of when
he was a mischievous young mouse.

The kids helped him up and copied his way of walking.
Like magic, a dozen Grandpas appeared.

Grandma fed sweet snacks to her sweeties.
The boys grabbed and gobbled. The girls dressed Grandma up.

After the girls were done, a lovely mouse as pretty as a fairy appeared.

Out of the kitchen wafted a sweet aroma.

To Mom, Auntie Jenny, and Auntie Lily, the festival was a happy but also busy time, as they were to cook the reunion dinner.

But strangely, Uncle Dom hadn't arrived yet.

Everyone sat around the long table, waiting.

It would not be a true family reunion if even one member were absent, so everyone waited patiently for Uncle Dom.

They waited and waited till it was dark.

Dad and Uncle John grew so anxious that they waited by the door.

Melvin and the other boys climbed up high, looking out into the distance.

Grandpa sighed deeply, and Grandma wept sadly.

They were all worried that bad luck had befallen Uncle Dom.

Finally, Uncle Dom showed up, but he was covered in wounds.
He had been chased and hurt by a cat.

Although Uncle Dom's tie was askew, his suit was torn, and his shoes were lost, he was still alive.

Dad tended to his wounds, Auntie Jenny washed his tie, and Mom and Auntie Lily mended his suit.

Uncle Dom was indeed a lucky mouse.

Finally, the whole family was here.

The reunion was affecti
come an end to the fest

Melvin hugged and kiss

and joyful, but there had to

relatives again and again.

the feast began.

Dishes were served, and t

After all the guests had finally left, Dad had his first taste of the yummy soup. He had been so busy entertaining guests that he hadn't eaten anything the whole day.

Mom smiled sweetly, her face radiating happiness as Dad complimented her cooking.

Melvin gave Dad and Mom a warm hug. What a lucky and happy mouse he was!

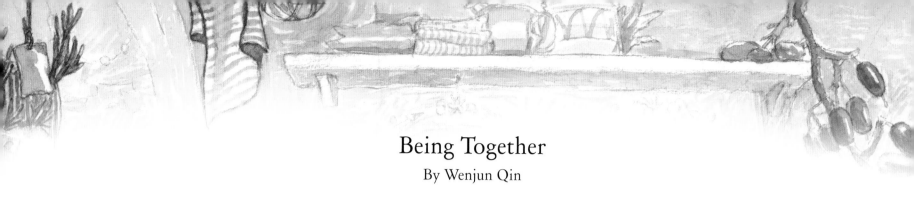

# Being Together
## By Wenjun Qin

The tone of this story is just like the world that Melvin sees — warm and affectionate but with a tiny bit of sadness.

On the eve of the festival, Melvin's family is happily preparing for the next day's reunion. Although Melvin is excited, he is worried. What if his relatives don't come?

The next day, his relatives arrive. The different families have different characteristics. Regardless of whether they come casually or well-dressed, they share the same purpose. They have come to meet their beloved relatives and to make up for the days they have spent apart.

Although the cellar is full of love and joy, everyone begins to worry about Uncle Dom. It will not be a true family reunion if one member is absent, so everyone waits patiently for him.

After a long anxious wait, Uncle Dom finally shows up. The sentence I am most satisfied with is: Everyone was now sitting around the long table, waiting for him.

Fortunately, the one they were waiting for appears. The longer they waited, the happier they are now. The accident helps them understand what family and happiness are. As long as a family member is safe, any wound will heal.

When people are together, they share love. Love is as warm as the sunlight.

I wish that people who love each other could be together for every festival.

Be together and be blessed.

## The Author

Wenjun Qin was born in Shanghai, China, in 1954. She is a famous Chinese children's book writer, having won over 50 awards in China and abroad. In 2009, she became the first Chinese writer to be shortlisted for the Astrid Lindgren Memorial Award. She was nominated for the 2002 Hans Christian Andersen Award. She has published 58 children's books and written more than 6 million words. To her, being a children's book author is the world's best job. She has a great understanding of what her readers like.

# The Magic of Love and Imagination

By Xiaoxuan Xu

When I was working on the pictures for this book, something funny happened. I had drawn the mice family during the day, while at night, I was awoken by noises. I was so scared in the darkness that I couldn't fall asleep. This reminded me of a similar experience from my childhood. I had been with another child, and in the darkness, I comforted her, "The mouse is just walking through our room, wearing leather shoes. Where do you think he's going?" I had to be the braver child.

What made me conquer my fear of mice, comfort the scared child, and go on to create a warm world of mice? I believe it must be a kind of magic.

The story that took place in the tiny cellar was an ordinary one, devoid of strong ups and downs. But it is these small things that become so wondrous and so important to Melvin and his family. It is love and imagination that made the author and me fall in love with Melvin and his family.

Love inspires love, curiosity sparks curiosity, and imagination protects imagination.

I hope this book will bring young readers a magical time.

## The Illustrator

Xiaoxuan Xu, who resides in Beijing, is an illustrator. She graduated from the Animation Department, School of Design, Jiangnan University. In 2011, she began illustrating for the Children Literature Magazine, which started her career as an illustrator. Since then, she has illustrated many children's picture books.

WHEN THE MICE FAMILY COMES TO VISIT

First Published 2019
ISBN 978-1-76036-089-4
Printed in China by Toppan Leefung Printing Limited
20th Floor, 169 Electric Road, North Point, Hong Kong

Thank you to Courtney Chow, Qinfang Gao and Marlo Garnsworthy (in alphabetical order) who were involved in translating and editing this book.

Our thanks also go out to Elyse Williams for her creative efforts in preparing this edition for publication.